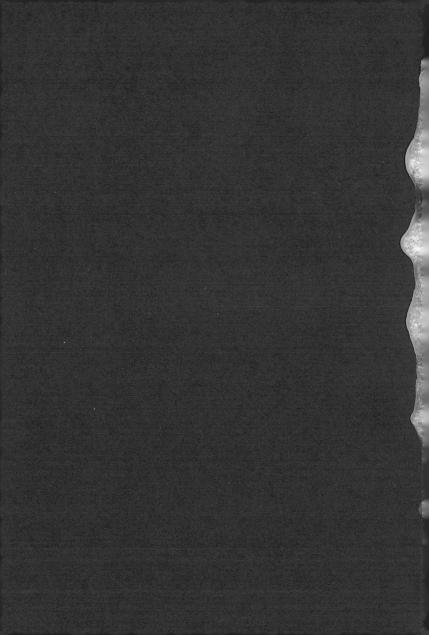

IN DARK PLACES

IN DARK PLACES

WYL MENMUIR

illustrations by Emma Butcher

National Trust

First published in the United Kingdom in 2017 by
National Trust Books
Heelis
Kemble Drive
Swindon
SN2 2NA

An imprint of Pavilion Books Group Ltd

ISBN: 9780707804422

Printed in LTC Kennerley by Palace Printers, Lostwithiel

This book can be ordered direct from the publisher at the
website: www.pavilionbooks.com. Also available at National
Trust shops or www.nationaltrustbooks.co.uk.

Acknowledgements

This publication is the result of a collaborative venture between National Trust Publishing and Falmouth University's staff, students and writer in residence, Wyl Menmuir.

Thanks are owed to Katie Bond and the National Trust, Patrick Kinsella and the South West Outdoors Festival, and to John Bond at Whitefox. Thanks also to Falmouth University's School of Writing and Journalism, to Niamh Downing, Anna Kiernan and Luke Thompson, and to the student publishing team led by Samantha Pentin, Benjamin G Wilson and Kate Williams. This team comprised Adriana Ciontea, Joanna Varandas, Alyanna Graham, Janina Zender, Anthony Sprouse, Holly Farr and Day Lilico. Thanks also to Emma Butcher for her illustrations, and to Steve Braund.

To Al, Jeni, Owen and Caitlin
The Adventurous Menvies

The brown stream falls into the rocks. Rich water draining in from the limestone heath. The hole is a pinprick eye staring out, wet in the undergrowth. Far above, two buzzards float on a thermal, one following the other. They trace an elliptic path across a sky that is cloudless and of the palest blue. On a branch in the brush by the cave entrance a small bird looks on, its head cocked.

They pushed aside the branches, shirts stained with sweat, ready to give up by the time they found it. They whooped and embraced and argued over who would get to go down first. They drew lots and the loudest one won. All four of them were loud, but he was the loudest. They sat around and unpacked sandwiches, pasties, fruit and chocolate. After they ate, they lay on the ground, stretched out, their limbs overlapping, looked up at the sky and imagined the depths they were to plumb. They were hazy in the sunlight, shimmering and smiling and young. Here's to being the first, the loudest one shouted and the others raised their water canteens and repeated his words. The first. They may have been the first. It is doubtful. They laid out ropes, helmets and torches, checked and rechecked them all before they descended the rocks, slick and calcifying. They abseiled into the depths, into the perfect darkness. Four of them, disappeared into cracks that opened long ago. They pressed themselves into thin fractures in the crust, just for the sensation of the weight of earth against their chests. Felt the rocks constrict around them and laughed as though it was new love. They crawled and swam in rivers and pools long buried. Pushed through sunken passages and were rebirthed into silent caverns that they filled with their shouts and laughter. They woke us with their heavy footsteps and their echoes, while, far above, clouds that were not there before gathered and rain began to fall.

There were once people who walked lightly. Who heard, in the space between their footsteps, reverberations and echoes of the fissures and caverns that lay below. Otherworlds and underworlds. Places that spoke to them. They did not dive into the openings they found, nor cross too far beyond the thresholds over which might spill a horde of monstrous cats, or ravenous birds, released for a short while onto the thin surface to feed. Depths into which one might be dragged and from which there was no return. They respected this was the case. Ventured no further than they needed. Things change though. It is the only truth.

I want the full works, the man is saying. We've come a long way for this.

The caves here are an ancient house in which no one has bothered to count all the rooms. A house to which there are many entrances and fewer exits. It is a house in which the rooms change shape and location, that flood and collapse, expand, contract, disappear entirely. In which the passage of time and water carves out yet more rooms to replace those that are now gone. Entire wings are cut off from one another, separated by water or by rock fall. The roof's

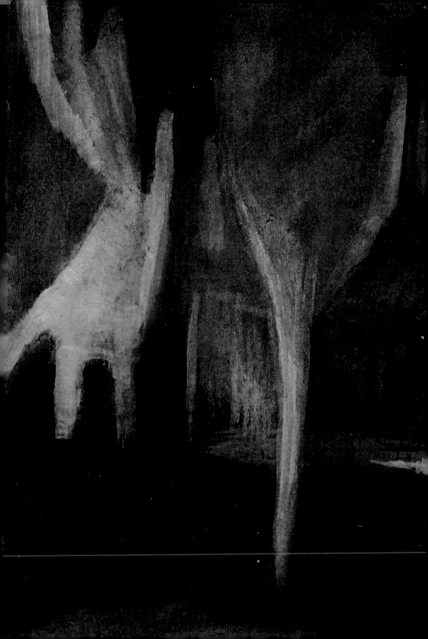

many domes and cupolas are polished into smooth whorls. There are ballrooms here too, state rooms and sunken parlours, forgotten attics and cupboards so small you can barely bury a child in them. It is a house in which arcuated corridors, striated and scalloped, confuse and mislead, run back on themselves or taper into paths too narrow to follow. There are signs at one of the entrances now. This entrance, close to the valley floor, has a café and an office that sells tickets. There is a man and a woman standing at the turnstile.

The full works? the boy selling tickets is thinking, as though he could throw in some extra caves now he knows it is demanded. The woman cringes. It is the height of summer and the queue is growing. The boy takes their money and asks the couple to stand to one side. They will be met at the gate shortly. The man and the woman stand close to one another but do not hold hands. After ten minutes, during which they read the signs on the walls, a young man with a beard arrives. The guide. He apologises for making them wait. There was a problem with a goat on the cliffs above. He is kind to the goats, this man, and the sheep too. He leads them back to safety. When the guide tells the man and the woman about the goat, he is met with blank stares. He ushers them away from the entrance to a small concrete block set into the cliff, where he hands them boiler suits, harnesses, wellingtons, helmets, head torches to put on. The woman seems confused by this. The man spends an age trying to fit his harness. He exchanges his glasses for contact lenses and he ends up dabbing dust into them. While he is making his eyes sore the woman is overheating on the balcony outside. We hear the word honeymoon. An angry word she repeats over and again in her head. The guide asks the man if he would like to leave his camera in the room. It will be safe there. The room will be locked. The man laughs and says the camera should be strong enough to take whatever they throw at it. They are hard to see in the light, these three figures. They are blurred and they only start to come into focus as they bypass the queue and are shown through a gate by the side of the turnstile. At the threshold they stand where the light filters in and the man holds forth about the skeleton that had been discovered in a small cavern just to the left of where they are standing. How these are the oldest human remains. He has read leaflets in their holiday cottage. He has looked it up online. The woman wonders whether her husband is aware the skeleton they can see is a plaster cast. She shares a look with the guide who smiles but says nothing and moves them on.

The plaster cast of his bones is confusingly similar though it is not the same as him at all. We remember when he arrived. It was a long time ago. The people who came then never went any further than this point. The point at which shadows start to eat away at the daylight. Well, few of them. He was not dead when he arrived, but he could not stand like the others. He was carried in and placed on the ground and left. He coughed and moaned and slept and dreamt and slipped in and out of consciousness as the night wore on and throughout the next day before he stopped moving. He was not the first to arrive, not by a long way. The living and the dead, brought and left. We remember a mother. She carried her son to the entrance. His head was caved in on one side and before she left, she asked us to help him, as though she thought there was something we could do. Before he died the boy lay on his back and watched the bats as they flitted in and out of the entrance and when it became too dark we showed him more images of bats to comfort him until his breathing became too quiet for even us to hear. And then there were long periods when they did not come. Still air. Creatures that walked quietly. The spring torrents. The movement of the rocks. Wearing away and building back up. Flooding and emptying. Ebb and flow. The slow shifting and rearranging of rooms in the darkness.

The couple move further in, away from the daylight. The man struts and points his camera at everything and talks to the guide with authority. The guide nods in the right places. The man ignores the curtain stalactites that glow softly in the halogen light and the small forest of ferns that have grown up beneath the lamps in niches in the wall. The woman sees them and lingers, taking them in. She likes the lights in the recesses best, the ones that hint at other places just out of reach. We remember the first lights. Burning sticks. Candles. Oil lamps. Lights on strings, like burning thread that runs through the labyrinth. We have heard that story too. They leave the lights on all the time now, even when they are not here. We sometimes make them flicker and watch the shadows dance on the walls.

As they pass them, the couple stare up at the pallets of cheese, unsure what to make of them.

Is this normal then? the man asks. The cheese, down here. It can't be hygienic.

He has read about this too, though he did not believe it, somehow. It does not fit with his image of the cave nor of what he is doing here. He will edit it out of the picture later. The guide explains the constant temperature in the caves makes them the perfect place to mature the cheese, but they do not linger. Further in, the guide pauses at a small offshoot and points out to them a feature in the rock.

If you part-close your eyes and tilt your head slightly, he says, you can make out the curve of a mammoth's tusk, and here the back, and its hind legs. It follows the curve of the rock.

They both stare at it and the man nods and says yes, he can see it.

I think it's unlikely, the guide continues.

The people who found it were looking for this, or for something like it. So, they found it. We see what we want to see, and if someone points something out to us and tells us it is there, we want it to be true, so we convince ourselves that it is. We create the story for ourselves. If there were carvings here, they've been long washed away by the floods.

She was with the university, the woman who discovered the mammoth. She saw herself as much a caver as an academic. She had examined the walls of almost every cave in the country that was known to have been inhabited. We heard the word Altamira as it repeated itself endlessly in her head. She was slow. Methodical. Sometimes she forgot what it was she was looking for and seemed to be feeling for something else in the rock. She cared for each of the tiny scars and nicks on the walls much as the guide cares for the goats. She inched along, sometimes stopping and staring, tilting her head to one side and then the other. She put a hand up to the rock face. Traced a tusk, the dome of a head and the curve of a back with the tip of her finger and we felt her excitement through the rock. She could see the carver, had already started to flesh him out in her mind, his life and habits, his hidden motivations. We had felt this before. It is palpable, this need to understand. We do not remember anyone having carved this here. But it has been a long time, so, perhaps.

Others stop to inspect the carving, to puzzle at it. It is busy in the caves today. When it is like this, we think about sending cats out. Thousands of them. Especially when the caves are full and the lights seem too bright and the noise builds until they are shouting over themselves. A little further on, the guide lifts a chain and they turn away from the families milling around on the main path. He asks the man and the woman to turn on the lights on their helmets.

They clamber up to the foot of a large

boulder, where they clip on to a safety line and make their way up a series of aluminium ladders that are roped to the rocks. We see her thoughts clearly here, away from the well-lit passage where everything is slightly fuzzy. They are just married. It is her first marriage. They were married on a cloudless day that marked the beginning of the hot summer and the day itself had seemed long to her. The photographer had complained that there was too much light and when she looked at the photographs later, she was inclined to agree. They looked washed out, their faces pursed, skin pale. They lacked depth. If someone had told her they were fakes, she might have believed them. The ladder shudders as they cross gaps that the guide tells them have names like Endless Drop and Bottomless Pit. If only he knew.

Isn't it dangerous? the woman asks.

It is the first time she has spoken since they entered the caves. The man laughs.

Here, the guide takes them to where the roof dips and they crouch and then crawl and then lie on their stomachs and pull themselves through, into the diminishing gap between the roof and the floor. They contort themselves through the passage, though the guide knows there is a way a few metres from them where they could walk and their heads would not touch the roof. There is a climb, a scramble through mud. They sweat and flush and their hearts race. When they emerge into the next chamber, they rest for a while as the guide tells them a story about a young man who went caving alone, who kept pushing on as the cave got narrower and narrower, as the passage tipped downwards and he pushed on with his arms out in front of him until there was no way forward and no way to get back. That he was found weeks later, wedged into the rock. He has told this story before.

We have heard a great many stories. Some of them we remember well, cannot dislodge.

Others lose their way. They disappear into the crevasses. Most of the stories we have heard were told close to the entrances, pieced together from whatever scraps were lying around, detritus and lies built up until they became as intransigent as the rock walls. Stories told by firelight, tentative explorations and explanations. Stories told by candlelight, when grand feasts have been assembled, tales of awe and of the sublime. Stories told by torchlight as cards were shuffled and bets placed. Stories told in dark places, whispered close in to another's ear. Confessions and stories to enlighten, to comfort, to seduce. And our favourites, the ones in which the teller does not even recognise what they are doing is telling a story at all. Those that took place a long time ago and those that are closer, they blend and converge, overlap and run on into each other. Perhaps it is because they are similar stories. The same ones, told over and again, in different voices. Some of the older stories degrade and grow increasingly vague. This is how we know they are older stories. Some we have forgotten entirely.

They scramble up over the boulders at the far end of the chamber and the guide points them towards a small gap in the rocks above. He will meet them at the top, he says.

Who will go first? The woman. She did not want to be here, although now she is, she feels the blood in her face and the sweat slick between her shoulder blades and she is glad she came. The gap becomes narrower and the way steeper and halfway up the climb she is convinced she will not get through. She holds herself still for a moment, breathes, kicks her feet against a narrow ledge she cannot see behind her and pushes. And she is moving through the space that a moment ago looked impassable. She squeezes herself through the crack and we feel her pulse race, the thrill of it. Below, the man rubs more dust into his eyes and curses. He starts to climb up towards the woman. We are tempted to compress the walls around him, just slightly. He comes to the push and can get no further and he claws at the rocks and kicks against the smooth walls.

You just need to jam one of your feet . . . the woman calls down to him. Do you need a hand? I could pull you through.

The man ignores her and continues to scrabble. His hands cast about, sweating and slipping on the rocks. He pants like a crow.

These stupid caves, he says and he pushes against the rocks again, his elbows out to the sides and his feet now swinging in space. He thinks no one else has heard him say this, though the woman hears it and the guide too. In the end, the guide comes round and pushes him up by his feet.

They come out at the top of the cave, having worked their way up the steep sides, and peer down into the dark. The guide explains to them what will happen next and asks again which of them will go first. The man pushes himself forward and the guide talks him through the abseil and he lets himself down in short jerky movements. Halfway, he hears a crash against the rocks below. The woman, when she comes to it, swings back off the ledge and abseils into thin air into the middle of the cave as though she is falling back onto a bed or into cool water. She lets out cord in long sweeps and her movements are confident, relaxed. The man does not notice when she lands beside him on the floor of the large chamber. He is trying to piece the camera back together and cursing under his breath. While he does this, the woman looks around at the boulders strewn across the floor and at the telephone on a box on the wall. They have both lost all sense of direction now. This always amuses the guide.

This is as far as we go, the guide says. Further on there are more chambers we know about. There are long passages that are permanently flooded. We're always finding new ones, small

openings, caves we've not explored yet. It's possible this network is just a small part of a whole system we've not even discovered or that it links to the other networks we know about.

Can we turn the lights out? the woman says. Just for a while? To see the darkness.

The man, who is now holding the broken housing of his camera, does not look keen. The guide asks them to sit on one of the boulders and then walks over to a set of switches on a board on the cave wall and turns the cavern's side lights off.

When you're ready, flick the switch on your head torches, he says.

The man's is the last to go out and when it does, the woman thinks maybe they have left a light on somewhere in the cave. There is a low purple glow, though she realises soon after that it is an illusion of the total darkness.

Hold a hand up in front of your eyes, the guide says. It's impossible to adjust to this.

The man starts to say something but the woman asks him to stop. Just to stop.

Can we sit like this for a while? the woman says. Without the light. Without talking. Just for a minute?

There was a man who came here once and did this. Sat in the dark. The one we called the hermit. He made camp just where the couple are sitting in now. Surrounded by boxes of books and candles and food. He sat and read, wrote stories to his daughter, paced the caves, turned the lights off and then on again. Sometimes he cried. Most of all he slept and when he was asleep we looked at him more closely. When he slept, he dreamt of flight. He had a problem with a cough. After a while he had a problem with time too. He started to feel like we do. We showed him images in the dark and he did not like this. And then he was gone. Four months. Blink of an eye, though we felt we had started to get to know him. Before he arrived, a group of men installed a yellow telephone. Bright yellow. Sometimes, in the night, we make it ring. It is one of the many things left behind, along with the strings of lights, tusks and flints, bones and mushroom spores, a wedding ring, a child's toy that was dropped into one of the deeper caverns and that lies on its back looking up into the darkness. And now shattered glass from the lens of the man's camera that he has trodden into the clay.

Most people seem to think they are opaque. In the darkness, though, they become clear. Luminous. Readable. The two men and the woman sit in silence and the woman tries not to listen to the sound of the two men breathing. She tunes into the faint echoes of the cave and thinks about the ones that are flooded. She thinks about swimming in a submerged lake in the perfect darkness. She can feel the silt between her toes as she kicks off the floor, the velvet water on her back and on her legs as she stretches them behind her, as she loses sense of place and time. Shapes dance in front of her and she knows she is projecting them, and it is beautiful. It is so dark she expects that if she looked hard enough she would see stars, constellations, galaxies in the blackness, as if she was not looking out at walls, but onto a firmament. She feels the darkness pouring into her.

It is then we show her. Just a single image. A negative. She blinks and it is gone. We show her the four of them, suspended, mid-solution. They are in one of the chambers we keep permanently flooded now. They do not touch the sides, not ever. We move them sometimes, just slightly, set off currents and eddies, tiny vortices in the still water. Ripple and fade. Two of them, the lovers, we keep close together. It seems right. They are locked in a slow dance in the water, cold cheek to cold cheek, while the other two look on.

It was not due to rain that day, so they weren't looking out for it. They were a mile or so in when the rain began and they had just decided to turn back when it started to flood. The kind of thing where the sky just opens up. They were young. Caving club types. We had seen many like them before, in other wings of this sprawling house. And when the water started to roll in, it rose quickly down there and cut them off where they were. When they realised what was happening, they moved towards each other rather than looking for an exit, as though collectively they were more protected. None of them said it, but the water trap was clear in their minds as they made their way back towards it. It had been a couple of metres when they made the dive the first time. The rain took the whole tunnel out and it flooded fast, and pushed them back towards the larger chamber. They knew, immediately. They knew. The tunnel was still flooding and there was no telling when it would open out again, so they did the only thing they could and swam. Down into the airless dark, back through the crawl hole through which they had emerged. And the rain continued, the trickle of water at the entrance now a cascade. Two tried to turn back, though by then it was too late for all of them. We watched them fight it, for longer than we would have thought possible, before they were still. Later, there were lights on the hill, flashing and pulsing. And a crowd of people turned up at a clearing by an entrance that was nearby though not the right one. Some went a way in. First one group, then another. We recognised the names they shouted. We recognised their need for an answer. A few days later, another crowd gathered outside the same entrance, and huddled in to hear what the robed man said over the wind. Afterwards they boarded the entrance up and later they replaced the boards with a metal door and secured it with a padlock.

We care for them like we cared for the others. Perhaps that is why we are here. To care for the ones who were left.

The guide asks the man and the woman to close their eyes and to cover the lamps with their hands when they turn them back on. The woman blinks several times. Each time she does, the image of the four cavers flashes onto the red canvas of her eyelids. She has accepted it.

When they are gone, and when the screaming children are gone and the elderly gentlemen who are on a tour of sorts too, and the students who talk in a language we recognise but cannot understand, we forget about the man and the woman for a while and watch the bats as they emerge from their caves and take back the space for themselves, balletic and swift. Their choreography is strange even to us. Even after all this time. The bats have been here the longest. In the evening, in the between times, they flit and dance, and at day they cluster and rustle, unfold and refold their paper wings. And under the heat of the cave lamps, the ferns continue to grow.

The caves are never empty for long. They cannot stay away from them, as though an itch that started a long time gone has just grown as the centuries have worn on, has built incrementally, as stalagmites grow. We recall being woken by voices at the entrance, dynamite blasts in the deep, the opening out of new chambers. We marvelled at the speed with which they did this. The talk of opening this cave out and extending this passage. Theorising. Mapping and sketching. On paper, the cave's thin fingers stretch out for miles. There is a passage just beyond this point. We can feel it, the ones with picks and dynamite, say, and continue their digging and blasting. Their voices echo in the chambers.

It is like this now, but it will return to the way it was before. A flood or a fall. The filling of the caverns with limestone deposits. To the way it will be after the swift passing of men.

And the slow drawing of a stalactite from a rock.

And the slow violence of water.

And the slower violence of time.